A STORY ABOUT ADOPTION

A Sister for Matthew

By PAMELA KENNEDY
ILLUSTRATED BY AMY WUMMER

gpKids™
Nashville, Tennessee

JJ

ISBN 0-8249-5527-7

Published by GPKids
An imprint of Ideals Publications
535 Metroplex Drive, Suite 250
Nashville, Tennessee 37211
www.idealsbooks.com

Color separations by Precision Color Graphics, Franklin, Wisconsin

Printed and bound in Italy by LEGO

Library of Congress Cataloging-in-Publication Data

Kennedy, Pamela, date.
  A sister for Matthew / by Pamela Kennedy ; illustrated by Amy Wummer.
     p. cm.
  Summary: When Matthew's parents decide to adopt a baby girl from China he has many questions, but by the time she arrives, he is excited about his new sister.
  ISBN 0-8249-5527-7 (alk. paper)
  [1. Adoption—Fiction. 2. Intercountry adoption—Fiction. 3. Brothers and sisters—Fiction.] I. Wummer, Amy, ill. II. Title.
  PZ7.K3849Sis 2005
  [E]—dc22
                         2005025473

10 9 8 7 6 5 4 3 2 1

Designed by Eve DeGrie

For Joshua, son of my heart. —P.J.K.

To Tatiana, who is smart and beautiful too! —A.W.

A NOTE TO PARENTS
By Vicki Wiley

The term *adoption* is usually associated with incredible happiness for the parents of the soon-to-be adopted child. For the other children in the family, however, there may be fear and apprehension that they do not understand and cannot express. Added to this apprehension, their parents quite naturally, and unconsciously, concentrate on the newly adopted child.

Parents understand that they must encourage the adopted child to discuss his or her feelings. The biological or previously adopted child, however, is expected to be understanding and accommodating to the new child despite possible insecurities about his or her own role in the family.

To ensure a smooth transition, take the time to discuss adoption with each child. You might approach the subject with the older siblings with nonthreatening questions such as: "Do you ever wonder about your brother or sister's adoption?"

To reassure the older child, begin the discussion with statements such as:

* "Now your role is as big brother or big sister, and that means . . ."
* "You are just as important and just as loved as your new brother or sister."
* In the case of a biological child: "If we had had a choice, we would have chosen you."
* In the case of an older adopted child, tell the story of how the older child was chosen.

Tell the newly adopted child, even before he or she can talk, the story of his or her adoption. Good ways to begin include the following:

* "Let me tell you how [or why] we chose you."
* "You are an important part of our family, even if you look different."
* "You are just as important and just as loved as your older brother or sister."

For the older adopted child, talk about his or her memories. Keep the good ones alive, while being patient and reassuring about any unpleasant memories.

Return to these conversations with both the adopted child and the biological child year after year. Welcome all questions and discussions from all of the children. And perhaps most importantly, encourage your children to view adoption as the way God completed your family.

Vicki Wiley holds a Master of Arts in Theology, with an emphasis on children in crisis, from Fuller Seminary. At present, she is Director of Children's Ministries at First Presbyterian Church in Honolulu, Hawaii.

M atthew, would you get the mail from the mailbox?"

"Sure, Mom." Matthew ran to the box and scooped out all the letters and magazines.

"Who is this letter from?" Matthew waved an envelope in the air. It had a stamp with a panda on it.

"Oh, that's the letter I've been waiting for!" She grabbed the letter, tore it open, and read it. Then she placed a small photograph on the table in front of Matthew. It was a picture of a chubby baby with straight black hair. The baby had round, dark eyes and was wearing a red shirt.

"Matthew, this is your new baby sister!" Mom said.

"Really?" Matthew picked up the photo. He looked at Mom.

Mom laughed, put her arm around Matthew, and squeezed him tight. "This little girl lives in an orphanage in China. We are going to adopt her and make her a part of our family. Isn't that wonderful?"

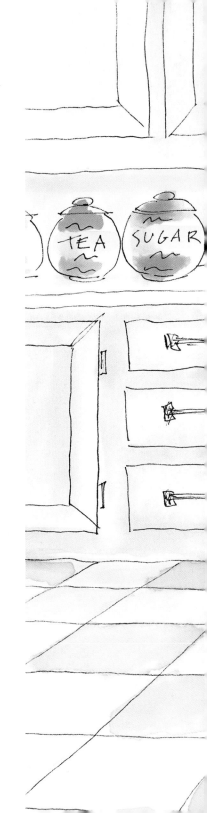

Matthew wasn't too sure it was wonderful. He liked things the way they were. His friend Jason had a little sister, and she was a pain. Matthew frowned. Maybe Mom didn't like things the way they were. Maybe she wanted a baby girl instead of Matthew.

"Would you like to take this picture of your new baby sister to show-and-tell tomorrow? You can share your news with all your friends."

Matthew shrugged. "OK," he said.

That night Mom got out the globe. She pointed to China. It was on the other side of the world. She said the baby girl's name was Mingmei and that it meant "smart and beautiful."

Matthew wondered how a fat little baby girl could be smart or beautiful.

At bedtime, Dad came in to read Matthew his favorite story.

"Why do people adopt babies?" Matthew asked.

Dad reached over and ruffled Matthew's hair. "There are lots of reasons, Matty. Sometimes it's because the Mommy and Daddy can't make a baby grow inside the Mommy. Sometimes they adopt babies because they want to give a home and family to a baby who doesn't have one. Sometimes they just want to share the extra love they have with another child."

"Do people ever adopt babies because they don't like the kids they already have?"

"Oh, no, Matty." Dad leaned down and gave Matthew a big hug. "We will always love you. No one could ever take your place in our family. Never, ever."

The next day, Matthew took Mingmei's picture to school. He shared it at show-and-tell. "This is a picture of Mingmei. She lives in China. It's all the way around the world from here. She's going to be my new baby sister."

The kids passed around the picture. Sara said the baby looked chubby. Erik wanted to know if she spoke Chinese. Jenny said she thought Mingmei was a pretty name. Jason said that Mingmei didn't look like Matthew.

When school was over,
Matthew's mom was waiting.
She was talking to Jason's
mother. Jason's sister was in her
stroller. She had red curly hair
and freckles just like Jason and
his mom. You could tell she
belonged to Jason's family.

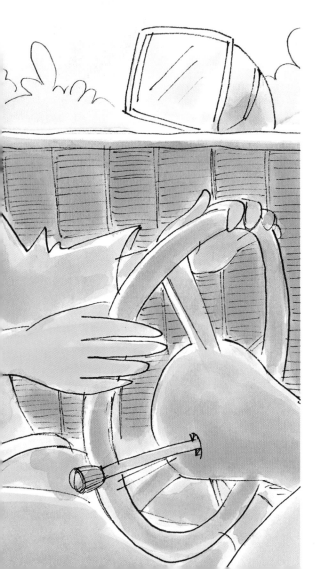

On the way home, Matthew said, "Mingmei doesn't look like us."

"No," said Mom. "But looking like someone doesn't make you a part of their family, Matthew. When you adopt someone into your family, they become part of your family forever, even if they don't look like you."

"Will we have to learn Chinese to talk to Mingmei?"

Mom laughed. "No, I don't think Mingmei can talk yet. But you can teach her. That's an important job for a big brother."

"How will Mingmei get here?" Matthew asked one day when he brought in the mail. He wondered if she would be sent from China in a big box and brought to their house by the mailman.

"Daddy and I will go to China to get her," Mom said. "We will be gone about two weeks. Grammy and Gramps will come and stay with you."

Matthew was glad Mingmei wouldn't be sent in the mail. Sometimes boxes got smashed. And it would be fun to have Grammy and Gramps come stay for a while.

"Will they be Mingmei's Grammy and Gramps too?"
he asked.

"Oh yes," Mom said. "When a child is adopted, she
becomes part of the whole family—aunts and uncles
and cousins and everyone!"

Finally, the day came for Matthew's parents to fly to China to get Mingmei. Grammy and Gramps and Matthew took them to the airport.

"We'll see you in two weeks!" said Mom and Dad. Grammy and Gramps and Matthew waved goodbye.

Matthew decided to make a "Welcome Home" present for Mingmei. He wanted to make her a book about how she came to be a part of his family. He asked Grammy to type the words on the computer and then Matthew drew the pictures to go with the words. This is the book that Matthew wrote:

Dear Mingmei, this is a book I wrote for you.

You were a baby in China.

Mom and Dad and I wanted to adopt you.

They went on a big plane to get you, and I stayed with Grammy and Gramps.

When you come to my house, I will be your big brother. Forever.

I will teach you stuff. I will take you to show-and-tell.

When you get bigger, we can have fun together.

I hope you like being in our family.

One day, Matthew and his grandparents went to the airport very early in the morning. Matthew saw Mom and Dad first. They were pushing a stroller with a baby in it. The baby had black hair and big, dark eyes.

Matthew leaned down in front of the stroller. He looked at Mingmei and said, "Hi, little sister."

Mingmei looked at Matthew for a moment. Then she smiled a great big smile. She had four teeth! She clapped her hands together and laughed.

Right then and there, Matthew decided that his new adopted sister was not only smart, she was beautiful too!

In Their Own Words

Pamela Kennedy

I live in Hawaii with my husband and our crooked-tailed, gray-and-white cat, Gilligan. Three days a week I teach at a school for girls in Honolulu. When I'm not teaching, I write. I have loved writing stories ever since I was in elementary school. Sometimes I make up pretend adventures, and other times I write about things that have really happened to me. *A Sister for Matthew* is a combination of imagination and real life. Over thirty years ago, my husband and I adopted our first son, Joshua, when he was only seven weeks old. Just like Matthew, I wrote a book for our son telling him all about the day he was adopted. I hope you enjoy reading this story as much as I enjoyed writing it. *Aloha.* —P.J.K.

Amy Wummer

I live in Reading, Pennsylvania, with my husband, Mark, and our three children, Jesse, Maisie, and Adam. I have loved to draw ever since I was a little girl. Each new project is a challenge, and every book, an adventure. I feel lucky to be having so much fun, and I truly enjoyed working on this book. The subject held special meaning for me. My little niece Tatiana, whom we call "Miss T," became part of our family three years ago when she was adopted by my husband's brother and his wife. Before coming to the United States, Miss T had lived in an orphanage near Siberia. She's just adorable, and we feel fortunate that she came to our family. —A.W.